NICE & BEAUTIFUL

KID'S FAVORITE

Coloring Book

COLOR ME at will

BY

John Thomas.J

TABLE OF CONTENTS

Space shade color

 RHOMBUS

Cylinder color shape

RECTANGULAR PRISM SHAPE

Color circle space

Color square space

Color empty space

INTRODUCTION

This book was written by **John Thomas.j** it's teach kid of begginner to know how to color and write which also expose their knowledge in to higher way of learning,color book is the book that bring moral intellectual idea for kid's,thus they need to discovered there talents or gift that God impacted to them.

CHAPTER 1

RECTANGLE: is the shape that has four angle if you colour me you will know that I'm bold and beautiful,I have space in me,I look like note

book which you are reading in
your class, my shape form
like bed,which you can sleep
on it,my rectangular
bed make me feel comfortable
and wake up with smile,color
me I will make u smile and
look nice.

CIRCLE

CIRCLE: is a round shape which bring beautiful motive color and shape,circle is a kid fast learning to drawing any image.I'm a circle

i formed like plate which they are using to eat,
I'm a circle i formed like bucket, which they are using me to bath every day.
I'm a circle i formed like pot which they use me to cook food every day.

I'm a circle i formed like football which they are playing me on the field groud.
 I'm a circle i formed like a cup, which they are using me to drink water.I'm a circle i formed like a moon,which am so bright in the night,people see me,they love me, Because I'm beautiful in the night.

I'm a circle i formed like a milk tin, which I full with nutrients.that is little I can explain about me, color me I will give u good smile.

I'm so beautiful in round shape .

TRIANGLE

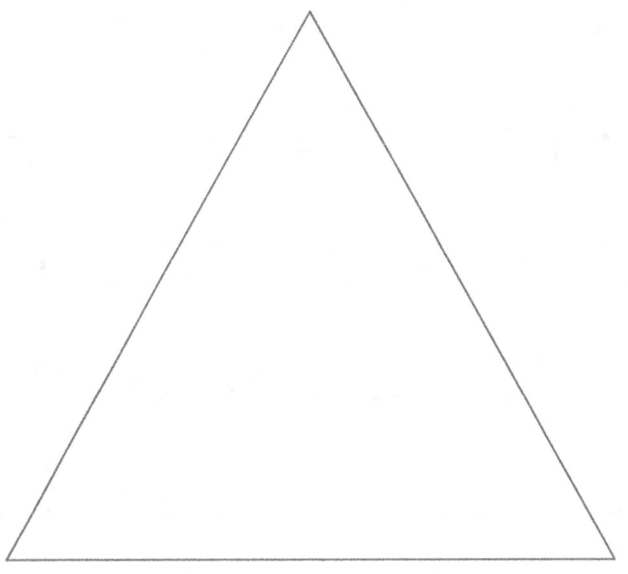

TRIANGLE: is the shape that have three angle,it's form like house,It also well design,u can design rectangle as a window shape.i I'm a Rectangle I formed like cave which they are living in the village,my Identity of rectangle shape bring more experience of three angle shapes.I'm scarce in shape to see other too look like me.i'm the only one made. i have three angle body you can formed me like house to live

in.color me am so beautiful.

BOX/CUBE

BOX/CUBE: is a shape that have 7 angle.it's called box which they are using to keep valuable things e.g document, jewelry, file, money etc.people like me because I save the secret belong,I'm wild inside to keep anything belong to them. Kid call me Mr big. because I'm big in shap.i give the them good structure, color me you and see that I'm not to big only am also bold and beautiful. box is well found in houses which they keep there valuable things.i am box, theycalled me MR.BIG.

CHAPTER 2
STAR

STAR: is a shape that have five angles,I called star

because am beautiful in the night on the sky people see they love me because am appearing on the sky in the night,I have song which beautify my status.

I'm a beautiful star,kids love me very well.!!!

Kids love me every night.

Once upon a time I bring

out story in the night ,,

never look for me any where.

just rise your head up,

I'm smiling to you down..

Space shade color

RHOMBUS

RHOMBUS: is a shape that

have a five angle,it's look

like kite, children like to play with kite,it's fly in the sky,if you color it you will see that it's beautiful,I love rhombus it beautiful to color with my taste.

CYLINDER SHAPE

CYLINDER SHAPE: is a shape that look like cup,many people like it. but it hardly for kid to differentiate it with cup, I love cylinder, my shape make me feel happy and I look beautiful, if you color me you will see that am not like cup but my structure it different,color is my priority, when am painted with your beautiful color you will smile to me and I will smile to you back because am now so beautiful than you.

RECTANGULAR PRISM SHAPE

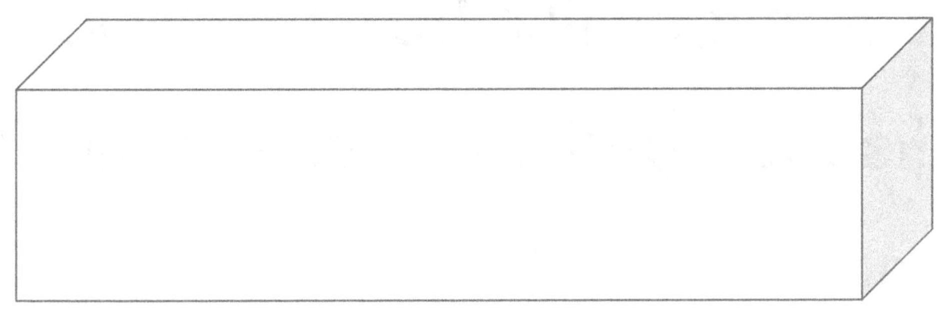

RECTANGULAR PRISM SHAPE:is shape that has seven(7) shape, it's also look like box cube or box, it also look like box, never be discouraged if you see cube and rectangular prism, because they want to look alike little.color me I will look like cartoon carton copy I'm also in horizontal in way,sleep and rest like you did in your bed.

Color circle space

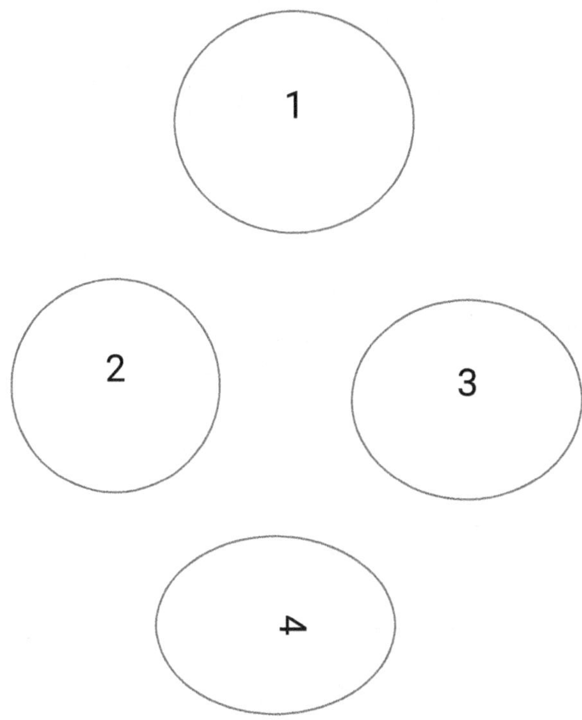

Color me I have four shape
to make me beautiful.

Color square space

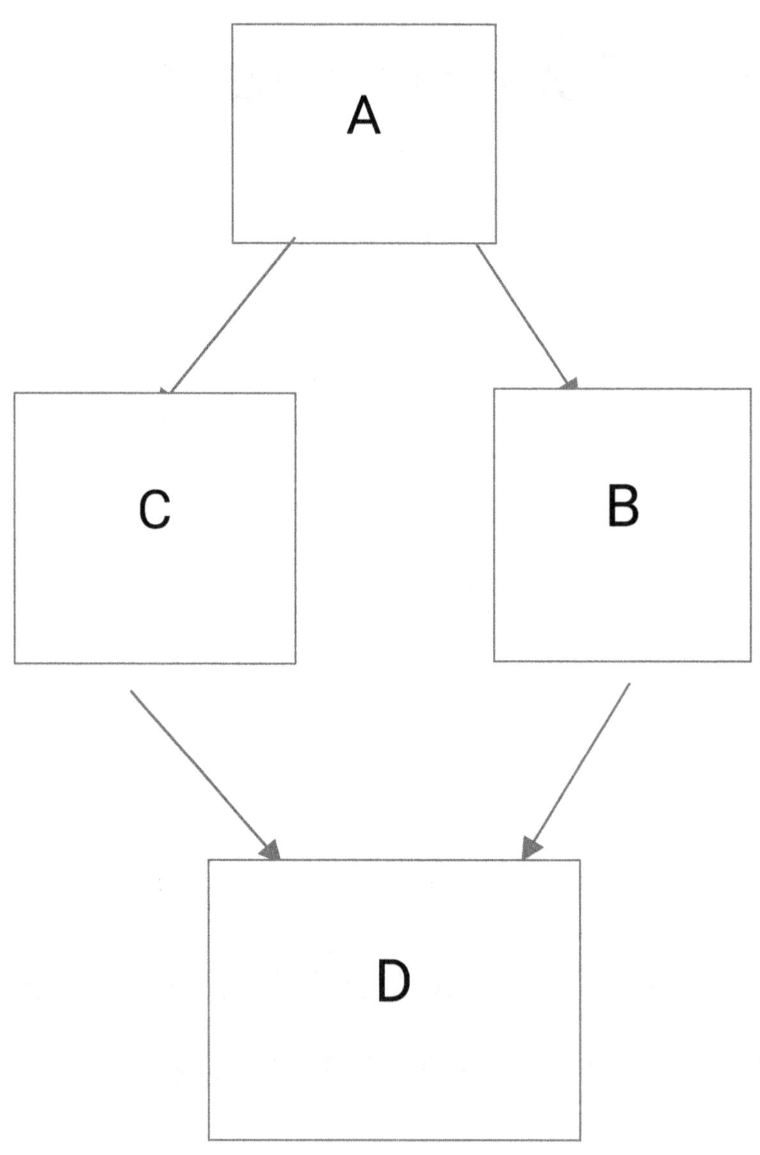

Color empty spac

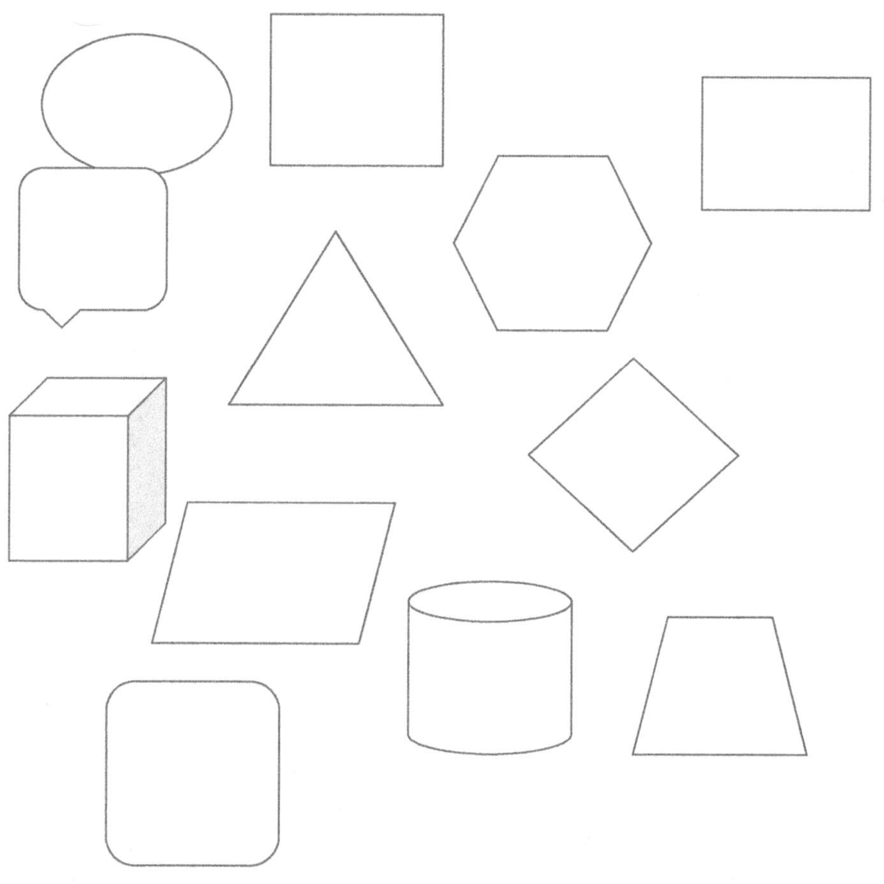